MAKING FRIENDS WITH MY EMOTIONS

IT'S OK TO BE DISAPPOINTED

THERESA EMMINIZER

PowerKiDS press

Published in 2025 by The Rosen Publishing Group, Inc.
2544 Clinton Street, Buffalo, NY 14224

First Edition

Editor: Theresa Emminizer
Book Design: Michael Flynn

Photo Credits: Cover, p. 1 kimberrywood/Shutterstock.com; (series background) Sergei Mishchenko/Shutterstock.com; pp. 5, 9 Prostock-studio/Shutterstock.com; p. 7 Len44ik/Shutterstock.com; p. 11 Krakenimages.com/Shutterstock.com; p. 13 Suzanne Tucker/Shutterstock.com; pp. 15, 19 fizkes/Shutterstock.com; p. 17 Photology1971/Shutterstock.com; p. 21 Dmytro Zinkevych/Shutterstock.com.

Library of Congress Cataloging-in-Publication Data

Names: Emminizer, Theresa, author.
Title: It's ok to be disappointed / Theresa Emminizer.
Description: [Buffalo] : PowerKids Press, [2025] | Series: Making friends with my emotions | Includes bibliographical references and index. |
Audience: Grades K-1
Identifiers: LCCN 2023054212 (print) | LCCN 2023054213 (ebook) | ISBN 9781499445022 (library binding) | ISBN 9781499445015 (paperback) | ISBN 9781499445039 (ebook)
Subjects: LCSH: Disappointment in children–Juvenile literature. |
Disappointment–Juvenile literature.
Classification: LCC BF723.D47 E46 2025 (print) | LCC BF723.D47 (ebook) |
DDC 155.4/124–dc23/eng/20231218
LC record available at https://lccn.loc.gov/2023054212
LC ebook record available at https://lccn.loc.gov/2023054213

Manufactured in the United States of America

CPSIA Compliance Information: Batch #CSPK25. For Further Information contact Rosen Publishing at 1-800-237-9932.

CONTENTS

Feeling Disappointed

Disappointment is the feeling of being let down by something or someone. When you're disappointed, your body might feel heavy. You might feel tired. Maybe your throat feels tight. Maybe your eyes fill with tears. That's okay! All feelings are natural. Even disappointment!

Why Does It Happen?

You might feel disappointed when you expect one thing to happen but something else happens instead. Say you're looking forward to a fun field trip at school. On the day of the trip, you're sick and can't go. You'd probably feel disappointed!

Feeling Let Down

Tasha's mom had promised to take her to a movie. Tasha couldn't wait! They'd eat popcorn and go to the big theater. But then, Tasha's mom called. She had to stay late at work. She couldn't take Tasha to the movie after all. Tasha felt crushed.

A Hard Feeling

Feeling disappointed can be very hard. It might even make you angry. There are lots of different reasons why you may feel disappointed. But it's important to know you won't always feel that way. Remember, feelings come and feelings go. This hard feeling won't last forever.

Dealing with Disappointment

Liam was disappointed. He had practiced and practiced. But on the day of the baseball tryouts, he wasn't picked for the team. Liam felt sad, angry, and **confused**. It wasn't fair! Liam hung his head. He wished this feeling would pass.

Let It Out!

Disappointment can be uncomfortable. You may want to hide your feelings or wish them away. Don't! **Ignoring** your feelings won't make them go away. It can even make you sick. Instead, let your feelings out. If you need to cry, cry! Crying can help you feel better.

More Ways to Cope

There are lots of ways to **cope** with disappointment. Try sharing your feelings with someone you trust. Or you could draw, paint, or write about how you feel. Movement is helpful too. When you're upset, moving your body can help you calm down.

You're Not Alone

Disappointment can be lonely. But remember, everybody feels disappointed sometimes. Even grown-ups! A safe adult will never be mad at you for sharing how you feel. It doesn't matter if they can't fix what's going on. Just sharing what you're feeling can help make it better.

Feelings Are Friends

Nobody likes feeling disappointed. But disappointment is a part of life. You don't have to hide your feelings or wish them away. Know you're not alone. This hard feeling will pass. Finding ways to express, or let out, your feelings will help!

GLOSSARY

confused: Unable to think clearly.

cope: Dealing with or working through your feelings.

ignore: To pretend something isn't happening.

FOR MORE INFORMATION

BOOKS

McAneney, Caitie. *I Talk to Cope.* New York, NY: PowerKids Press, 2023.

Wood, John. *Sam the Sloth Feels Sad.* New York, NY: Windmill Books, 2020.

WEBSITES

Kids Health
kidshealth.org/en/kids/talk-feelings.html
Learn how to name and talk about your feelings.

PBS Kids
pbskids.org/video/daniel-tigers-neighborhood/3068822559
Watch this video about how Daniel Tiger deals with disappointment.

INDEX